THE BOY
WHO SAILED THE
OCEAN IN AN
ARMCHAIR

LARA WILLIAMSON

USBORNE

For my family, with love

First published in the UK in 2015 by Usborne Publishing Ltd., Usborne House, 83-85 Saffron Hill, London EC1N 8RT, England. www.usborne.com

Text © Lara Williamson, 2015

The right of Lara Williamson to be identified as the author of this work has been asserted by her in accordance with the Copyright, Designs and Patents Act, 1988.

Photography: Fish © RKaulitzki/Thinkstock; Origami star © humback/ Thinkstock; Snail © dedalukas/Thinkstock; Armchair © Zastolskiy Victor/ Shutterstock

Illustrations © Usborne; How to Make a Paper Crane text and illustrations © Usborne.

The name Usborne and the devices 🎈 🌐 are Trade Marks of Usborne Publishing Ltd.

A CIP catalogue record for this book is available from the British Library.

ISBN 9781409576327   JFMAMJJ SOND/15   03225/1

Printed in the UK.

ONE

My name is Becket Rumsey and there are lots of important people in my life who I talk to every day. For starters: my seven-year-old bug-collecting brother, Billy, is one of them (although he talks nonsense ninety-nine per cent of the time – and the other one per cent? *Utter* nonsense). Dad, who delivers fish from The Codfather van, is another. Mainly he talks about haddock but I can live with that. Ibiza Nana, she's my grandma and she always rings for a chat from Spain. And then there's Pearl, Dad's girlfriend, I talk to her a lot and Pearl's good at listening. Plus, she gives great hugs and tells us she loves us to the moon and back, which is at least

768,800 km of love. I know this because Billy made me check. In fact, Pearl's almost a mum to Billy and me. I say "almost" because the one important person in my life who I don't get to talk to at all is my real mum.

My mum died when I was four. Not being able to talk to her is the hardest thing. Harder than trying to pat your head and rub your stomach at the same time. I don't remember a lot about when Mum died but I know she went off to hospital to have Billy and she never came back. And I never said goodbye to her. Okay, being totally truthful, at the time I didn't think saying goodbye was all that important. I mean, you're four and it's just a word, like "farm" or "zoo" or "dog". But now, at this very moment, I'm thinking "goodbye" is the most important word of all.

You see, it is eleven thirty on the Monday night at the beginning of half-term and I'm sitting in my dad's fish van outside a hairdressing salon called Crops and Bobbers. Dad is telling Billy and me that we've left our house at Honeydown Hills for good and we're moving into the flat above this hairdresser's, just the three of us. We're not to worry about leaving Pearl behind and, no, we don't need to worry about saying goodbye to her. She'll understand. No, we're not to ring her.

At first, I'm confused with a capital Z (so confused

I can't even spell, that's how confused I am).

Not say goodbye to someone so important for the second time in my life?

Not say goodbye to Pearl?

Dad's having a laugh.

Only Dad isn't having a laugh. His face is harder than dried-up breakfast cereal left in a bowl. If I could drive I'd go straight back to our house and Pearl. Tell her Dad has lost his marbles – in fact, that his marbles are so lost they're probably floating around in a galaxy far, far away. Pearl would welcome us back and say it doesn't matter that we didn't say goodbye because this isn't goodbye at all. It's hello. She'd bring us straight inside and let us play with her tubes of paint (because Pearl's an artist). She'd say she loved us all the way to the moon and back again and give us the biggest hug and we'd say we didn't actually go to the moon, just to Eden, but we're so glad to be back again.

When I tell Dad we should go back to Pearl, his mouth drops into an easy O. "You," he mutters, scratching the koi carp tattoo on his arm, "are not going back to say goodbye or anything else. You do not need to say it."

Well, my dad is a prawn short of a prawn cocktail.

"Plus there is the little matter of us being at our new flat already and it being the middle of the night. I can't be travelling all over the place at this time with two children," Dad says, forgetting that he's just done exactly that. Because about an hour ago he woke us up, threw all our stuff into boxes and strapped Mum's favourite armchair onto the top of the van beside the plastic one-eyed cod. When we asked Dad where Pearl was he said she'd gone out and then he shooed us into the van and we zoomed away as if we were in the Grand Prix. Although I don't think a van with a giant cod on the roof could enter. "Anyway, this is our new life now. We're going to be living by the seaside and this is our home." Dad points up at the flat as if he's the Wise Man from the East pointing at a star.

Living by the seaside? Our new life? I blink back my confusion. What was wrong with the old life? You can't just throw away old things like that. Otherwise we'd have slung out Ibiza Nana a long time ago. Okay, so saying goodbye doesn't seem all that important to Dad, but he's nuts if he thinks it's not important to me. Well, I'm going to do something about this. In fact, I'm not going to say goodbye to Pearl at all. What I'm going to do is contact her and bring her here to live with us. Yes, that's what I'll do.

But now I'm thinking about goodbyes, it reminds me of Mum and suddenly saying goodbye to her is what I

8

want more than anything. So the other thing I'm going to do is say goodbye to Mum, because I *can't* bring her here to live with us. No matter how much I wish I could.

"Okay, Dad, you're the boss," I say, saluting. This is what I call "the bluff". Pretend to Dad that I agree with whatever he says when really I don't agree with any of it and I'm going to do something about it.

By the way, Dad isn't the boss in our house at all. That was Pearl. Not that I'm saying she went about being all bossy-boots to everyone, but she liked things done her way. Like, even though it was our house that she moved into, she wanted to decorate it in her style. Pearl was very stylish though, so it was okay. She wore her hair in a bun secured with a paintbrush and these long floaty velvet coats that swished the floor, and when she wanted you to do something she'd smile and you'd want to do it for her because she was so lovely. In the end everyone wanted to do what Pearl asked. So, you see, Dad isn't the boss at all and that's why I'm going to be the boss on this – take control of the situation and bring Pearl back to us.

"Yes, Becket Rumsey," says Dad, running his hand over his bald head. You know Dad means business when he starts using my full name. "You're quite correct. On this, I am the boss. What I say goes."

"Yes, Stephen Rumsey," I reply, thinking that Dad has had a funny turn.

To be honest, Dad has had a few funny turns recently so I shouldn't really be surprised. For the past two weeks he has been extra quiet, plus he'd leave for work early and get home late. Pearl said she didn't believe he had to work so hard. She got angry about it. Dad would laugh and say she was giving him a haddock. That was him joking about. But Pearl didn't like it. She'd say fish aren't funny. Obviously she doesn't know the joke about the fight at the seafood restaurant where four fish got battered. Fish *are* a bit funny. In the end, Dad didn't bring fish home for our tea any more and he didn't talk about them so much.

Anyway, what I'm trying to say is, looking back on it...Dad hasn't been Dad for the last few weeks.

In fact, looking at him now, standing in front of our new flat, I'm not sure who Dad really is.

Okay, so we're here, a few minutes away from the ocean, and standing in front of a blue blistered door to the right-hand side of Crops and Bobbers hairdressing salon. Dad says, "This is it," and checks out my watermelon-slice-wide super smile. I think he's impressed that I'm so happy with all these changes. What he doesn't realize is this: it is the smile of a boy who is going to sort out everything. It is the smile of a boy who thinks his dad has gone completely bananas and the only thing left to do is pretend to be as bananas as him.

Billy pipes up that this flat isn't really our new home so it must be my birthday present. He lifts his finger and makes a home for it inside his nose, before jiggling it around like beads in a kaleidoscope.

Sweet Baby Cheeses! My entire family is bananas now. As if! Dad is not going to buy me a flat. I mean, I was just hoping for a life-size skeleton on my birthday, like any eleven-year-old boy. Though imagine if the flat *was* my new den, like Billy says: a place where I could store all my medical encyclopaedias. Imagine if Dad was investing in the future, knowing I'll need a special place where I can work in peace to find a medical cure for the heebie-jeebies...

Okay, this is ridiculous. I'm going as bananas as them.

"Why do you think I'd buy Becket a flat?" asks Dad, his eyes ping-ponging from Billy to me. "Anyway, it's not your birthday until next Monday." Dad says it like I don't have a clue when my own birthday is. "What parent would buy their child a flat as a gift anyway?" continues Dad, ushering us closer to the blistered door.

"A rich one?" I reply.

"Pffttt…" says Dad. "There's no money in fish." He points at a name on the buzzer. "Come here, Becket. Look at this. I haven't got my glasses on. What does that say? Is it Cat Wom…" Dad runs his finger over the illuminated button.

Holy smokes! "It is!" I exclaim. "Are we going to be living next door to Cat Woman? I can't believe it." At that point Dad pushes the button and even though he takes his finger off sharpish it keeps buzzing.

The lady who opens the door looks nothing like Cat Woman. For starters, she isn't wearing cat's ears or a funny mask. Although, to be fair, I might have actually wet my pants if she had been. Cat looks us up and down and then up again, as if she's watching some vertical tennis match. Billy tries to hide behind my leg as Cat gives Dad the key to our new flat and then asks us to follow her inside. Once up the staircase, Cat points to Flat A. "That's me." And then Flat B. "That's you. I own the hairdressing salon below. Come in for a cut at any time." She looks at Dad's bald head. "Maybe not."

Meanwhile, Billy is muttering over and over, "I think we should go home now." Wise words from young Billy;

12

quickly ignored by old Daddy. I feel Billy's cold little hand slip into mine and he gives me a squeeze. Okay, so it feels like he's milking a cow, but I know it's his secret way of asking me if everything will be okay. Call it a sort of code if you will; like the Enigma Code I learned about at school, only a billion times less complicated. This way we can "speak" to each other without actually moving our lips. It started a long time ago, when Billy came home from the hospital and he would grip my hand and I would squeeze his.

This time, even though I squeeze Billy's hand back, I don't actually believe everything *is* okay.

Billy whispers, "Why have we run away from home? Why isn't Pearl here? This is very much a mystery and we have to solve it."

"I know," I mumble back, "exactly what I was thinking."

Billy squeezes my hand again, but more urgently this time.

I squeeze his hand back.

Then I remember that he picked his nose.

TWO

I thought it would be me taking control of getting back in contact with Pearl. That it would be me who was the boss. I mean, I'm the eldest and it goes without saying that I am the most intelligent person in the family. But only the very next morning after we'd arrived at the flat, it was Billy who said we must text Pearl because that is how we would get her back. Annoyed that I hadn't thought of it, I reminded Billy that Dad had said we weren't allowed to ring Pearl. Feeling smug, I waited to hear what bright idea Billy had next. Bright ideas are not Billy's thing, you see.

Okay, so a minute later I realized bright ideas *are*

Billy's thing. "I'm not *ringing* Pearl," scoffed Billy. "I'm *texting* her. It is very different." Sometimes Billy is so daft he actually goes full circle and becomes a complete mastermind.

I hand Billy my mobile phone and he begins punching in his message. His eyes glittering, Billy says, "She'll text us straight back. Just you wait and see." No word of a lie, we wait and we wait. I look at Billy's message to make sure it has been sent and it has.

It's BiLly AND BECKET. We miS u. wee r here in Eden. COMe BaK 2 us. Pleese ANnswer. ☺

We wait a bit longer for a text back. I grow tired of waiting and start picking the fluff from my belly button. It is something to do and it's a lot better than staring at our new bedroom. Last night, Dad said he hoped we wouldn't mind sharing. He said it would be cosy. He smiled. I didn't. Dad brought Mum's armchair up from the van and put it in the corner of our new room. He said it belonged with me. When he'd gone to get the rest of our stuff from the van I sat in the armchair for ages and closed my eyes, wishing I was back at home. Then I wished Mum could come back to me even if it was only for a minute. Truth is, closing your eyes and wishing does nothing because when I opened them again I was still in a strange bedroom that smelled of mushrooms and Mum was still gone.

When we've waited fifteen minutes and I have enough fluff to make a home for a baby dormouse, Billy insists on sending another text. Well, I don't see what harm it could do, because maybe Pearl hasn't seen the first one. It's still quite early in the morning and Pearl doesn't usually get up much before nine. And I think about Ibiza Nana, who always says "The more the merrier" (particularly when she's talking about sherry). So I think the more texts we send, the more Pearl is likely to reply and the merrier we'll be, so I let Billy send a second one.

No answer.

Billy sends a third text.

No answer.

Billy sends a fourth text.

No answer.

Billy sends a fifth text.

At this point I have to stop Billy because once you've

done the poop emoji there's nowhere else to go. Pearl is clearly not going to send us an emoji in return. Reluctantly, I tell Billy we've got to knock it on the head, because Pearl's as silent as a burp in space. There will be another way to get her attention, I tell him. We just have to give it some thought. While we are giving it some thought at the breakfast table Dad tries to tell us how much we're going to love living here.

"If you cross the road you're straight into the park and there's a pathway that leads down to the harbour. Sometimes you can see seals there," says Dad. "And there are a lot of little fishing boats that take you out on expeditions to the ocean. Plus, we can spruce up this flat and make it really homely. We just have to pull together to make it work."

"The old house worked," I reply. I pause. "Why are we here, Dad? Why have we run away? Why didn't we bring Pearl with us?"

Dad doesn't answer.

Later that day, Billy has obviously given the matter of getting Pearl's attention some thought, because he hands me a rectangle of paper and says, "This is my business card."

I stare at it with a mixture of shock and admiration.

BILLY SPI
Miseries solved
Dead people found
Missing people found
Cawl - 0123456789

"It's interesting." I raise my eyebrows so high they're doing the eyebrow trapeze. "There are a few spelling mistakes." Giving Billy back the scrap of paper, I return to my book on parasites.

"No one is hiring me for my spelling," huffs Billy.

"No one is hiring you at all, Billy," I retort, reading about how pinworms can be detected by sticking tape to your bottom. "You're not a spy, Billy Rumsey." I turn the page to ectoparasites: bedbugs, head lice, fleas, ticks.

"Oh, yes I am." Billy sniffs dramatically. "And I've been thinking that Pearl must be dead."

Exasperated, I set the book straight down. Seeing he has my full attention, Billy continues, "Because when Dad brought the boxes up from the van there was a box of my stuff, your stuff, Daddy's stuff and Mummy's stuff. There was no box of Pearl's stuff. And..." Billy inhales and his chest puffs up. "Daddy doesn't talk about Mummy much and she's dead and when I wanted to talk about Pearl Daddy didn't, so I thought she might be dead too."

What kind of logic is this? Billy says he thought that maybe Pearl had e-clam-say-what. "Because Mummy had that and she went away and never came back and that was because of e-clam-say-what. And then Daddy was sad and didn't talk about it and Mummy was completely dead like that spider you whacked with your medical book called *Pop My Pimple*. And so I got to thinking Pearl must be dead too because Daddy seems sad and doesn't want to talk about it."

Eventually, when I find my tongue (despite it being in my mouth all along), I repeat that Pearl isn't dead. Mum had eclampsia and you only get that when you're pregnant, and it's very rare indeed that you will die from it. I tell Billy to trust me because I know all the medical facts about everything, which I do.

You see, I've wanted to be a doctor since I saw a man on telly pressing his lips on a plastic dummy. Dad said he was doing mouth-to-mouth resuscitation and heart massage and it would save lives. To be fair, it wasn't like any massage I'd ever seen. Once, Ibiza Nana asked me to massage the bunions on her feet and I didn't put my lips anywhere near those. Anyway, after that TV show I wanted to save lives more than anything.

Billy shakes his head and his dark curls spring about in different directions. "Well, okay, if Pearl's not dead then, smarty-pants, and we can't ring her, then that means Pearl is officially missing, like the sword from my toy pirate."

"Oh," I reply, hiding the sword inside my parasite book where I was using it as a bookmark. I pause before tilting my head. "...Kay. Let's just say you're right and we set up a spy agency – then we have to decide who the boss is, the person making all the decisions." I am so certain it should be me that I barely listen as Billy says he wants to be that very famous secret agent that everyone loves.

"James Bond," I mutter, turning to page sixty-three: hookworms.

"Perry the Platypus," Billy replies.

We spend the next twenty minutes in our bedroom setting up the spy agency. Billy says the room might be stinky and cold but it will do until we get somewhere better. I have a feeling that we're not going to get anywhere better but I don't tell Billy. First decision for the agency: what we should call it. Billy says "Billy Spy". I say that's boring and ask if it took him ten seconds to think of the name. Billy says it took him five. I offer "I Spy!" I don't mind saying that mine is the best and beats Billy Spy hands down.

Billy shakes his head like a person weary of dealing with a brother from Planet Moronic. "We have no time for games of I Spy." Straight away, he trots over to the corner of the bedroom and brings a pencil and another piece of paper out of his box of belongings.

"I Spy is a name for the agency, you muppet," I explain, rising from the bed and looking out of the bedroom window. Chip papers like tiny ghosts float across the pavement below and seagulls parade up and down the rooftops nodding to each other. This isn't where I'm supposed to be, I tell myself. I should have woken up in my own bedroom this morning. I drop the curtain and turn back, watching as Billy's pencil moves furiously up and down on the paper. "Or what about the Secret Network of Observations, Operations and Probing? SNOOP for short." It's genius, I tell you. I only just stop short of patting myself on the back.

Obviously, Billy does not recognize my genius

because he thinks about this name for a few seconds and then declares that it's "okay". It'll do for now, until he thinks of something much better, like Billy Spy. So, for the moment, we are members of SNOOP and, as members, Billy suggests we need to make secret name badges so we can recognize each other. When I say we're brothers so it's not that tricky recognizing each other, Billy says SNOOP members must not talk of their relatives.

After five minutes of drawing, my badge design is finished and I say I'd like to see Billy's efforts.

"I didn't draw a badge," exclaims Billy. He tuts and shakes his head like a dog with an ectoparasite in its ear. "If we had a badge with our name on, people would realize we are spies and no one is supposed to know."

"So what were you drawing then?" I sigh, not bothering to point out that he suggested making badges in the first place.

That's when Billy assumes his full height, which isn't anything to shout about since he takes after Dad on that, and wafts the piece of paper under my nose. "Is it a tissue?" I ask, only for Billy to tell me it's actually a letter and, what's more, it's a letter to Pearl. "I have said we miss her and she should come and live with us in—"

"Pies?" I snort, reading it.

"Peace," says Billy. "I made a spelling mistake – and anyway, Daddy would love to live in pies."

I tell Billy that maybe his idea about posting a letter to Pearl isn't such a bad one. She may not answer our texts but this could be the next best thing. I'm so on board with this idea that I start making plans of how we can find the nearest postbox. Maybe even sneak a stamp from Dad's wallet, because that's where he keeps them. Just behind the photo of Pearl and us.

Billy smiles at me like an evil egghead, his eyes narrowing. "Oh, Becket," he mutters. "We are not *posting* this letter. No, we are *hand delivering* it." That's when Billy says this is our very first SNOOP secret mission and I must choose to accept it. As Billy sets the letter down and begins to rummage around in his box of belongings, I say it's not much of a choice but I do choose to accept it anyway. "Found it," yells Billy with delight written all over his face (in invisible ink, obviously). He straightens up again and I realize he's holding a balaclava big enough for Mr Potato Head, knitted by Ibiza Nana. He pulls it on. "Mmmm disgggussse."

"Huh?"

Billy realizes it's on back-to-front and turns it around. "Phew! I wondered why the lights went out. It's my disguise. Now it's your turn."

Swallowing back my laughter, I say I can't fit in the same balaclava. Nodding, Billy produces my disguise from his box.

"No way am I going as a werewolf," I say, staring at it.

"I see," replies Billy, chucking it back in the box. "You are right. This rubber mask is too much like your real face. You need a different disguise." With that, Billy is back to rummaging around. The white woolly hat with ears that he throws at me next isn't much better. Who wants to go from a wolf to a sheep? When I think about protesting for the second time, Billy says I mustn't talk because he is coming up with SNOOP's plan of action, because spies must be organized and make very detailed plans.

After a few minutes of writing it down on paper, Billy shows me his very detailed plan:

THE PLAN

FLAT IN EJEN → (we are here)

we go from here to there

PEARL IN HONEYDOWN HILLS
(she is there)

Gobsmacked by the plan, and not in a good way, I tell Billy that getting from here to there isn't the actual problem. The actual problem is getting Dad to *let us* get from here to there. "We need to persuade Dad to let us out first," I say, my knitted ears wobbling as I tilt my head. "And," I add, "we need to think up a really good excuse or Dad will see straight through it. Or my name's not—"

"Shaun the Sheep?"

Dad looks a bit confused when I tell him Billy and I need to go play football straight away and when Dad opens his mouth to protest I make sure to promise we'll be back in time for tea. Dad thinks for a second and then asks if we mean at the park he mentioned across the road and I nod and then give Billy the little secret spy wink we'd discussed not more than two minutes ago in the bedroom. Billy grins and asks me if this park has a giant curly-wurly slide that makes your belly feel bubbly.

"Um...not sure." How would I know when I've never been there before? I wink at Billy again. You know, that secret spy wink that says we're in the middle of a SNOOP secret mission.

Anyone would think Billy hadn't been there when we discussed it, because now he is bobbing up and down like a jack-in-the-box on a trampoline. "Does the park have a sandpit? All the best parks have a sandpit. With hidden dinosaur bones under the sand." Billy is so excited now he's clutching his stomach and Dad is telling him to keep calm.

For Pete and Paulette's sake! "I don't know if it's got a sandpit," I say very slowly, making sure Billy understands. Right now, I'm secret-spy winking so much my eyelid thinks it's having a workout with a personal trainer – and *still* Billy doesn't get it. "We're playing football, aren't we, Billy?" *Wink-wink-wink*.

"Does the park have...? Does the park have...?" Anyone would think Billy was choosing a pick 'n' mix of what he'd like in his ideal park. In the end I just tell Billy the park has everything: super giant slides that make your tummy feel like you've eaten popping candy, swings that go so high your feet touch the clouds, roundabouts that go so fast that when you step off you immediately fall over...and dinosaur bones? Pah, not just bones: a real stegosaurus.

I think I might have laid it on a bit thick because Dad scratches the koi carp tattoo on his arm and says, "There aren't any real dinosaurs, Becket." Dad has

26

forgotten about the teacher I had in Year Four – he was a bit of a dinosaur. "And it's a bit cold out there," adds Dad. Billy replies that we have hats. He's already wearing his balaclava and I'm apparently disguised as a load of fluffy cotton wool, so the fact we have hats is obvious to any fool with eyeballs, which counts Dad in. Dad's still unsure about us going out when we've only been in the flat for less than twenty-four hours. That's when I tell Dad it's important for us to explore our surroundings and we can't be stuck in the flat any longer. "We'll get scurvy," I add quickly, and I offer to go and find my medical book that explains all the symptoms. I promise Dad there's quite a long list.

Dad's mouth slackens. "Um, nah, you're all right," he says. "But where's the football, because I didn't pack it in any of the boxes?" Dad shakes his head and says he hopes I'm not pulling the wool over his eyes, which is ridiculous since I'm the one with the wool pulled over mine. Dad repeats the question.

The football? To be honest, I hadn't thought of that. Thrown into a panic I look at Billy and he looks at me and after a few seconds of looking at each other I realize that this isn't getting us anywhere and I have to think of a clever response and fast.

"Er...we don't need one because we're playing

invisible football." That was some sort of response, but clever it wasn't.

"Right," says Dad, rubbing his eyelid and easing back into the sofa. "Why do you need to wear a sheep on your head to play invisible football?"

"I thought it was better than a werewolf," I reply.

Ah.

Eventually, after Dad says he supposes he could pop down to Crops and Bobbers and chat to Cat while we're out and ask her about things to do in the area and after about one million rules about what we can and can't do and when we have to return, we escape from the flat. The first SNOOP secret mission to find Pearl is a go-go.

Once we're outside I explain to Billy that we're not actually going to the park at all and there's no such game as invisible football and that it was just an excuse to get out without making Dad suspicious. Well, Billy is clearly not impressed by this because he kicks me on the shin.

"What's that for?" I howl.

"It's an invisible tackle," mumbles Billy through the balaclava. "And it's for making me think I was going to the park."

We wander across the road; two boys, one in a balaclava and one a hobbling sheep. Eventually Billy asks, if I'm so clever, then how are we going to get back to our old house in Honeydown Hills?

"WE'RE GOING TO CATCH THE BUS," I shout, gesturing to the bus stop opposite us. This morning, when I was looking out the flat window, I noticed the bus that passed our street was going to Honeydown Hills. So, even if I say so myself, I think I might be the master spy here. "WE WILL CATCH THE BUS RIGHT NOW," I yell.

"No need to shout," mutters Billy. "I'm wearing a balaclava, I'm not on Pluto." Yes, but I swear his brain is on another planet.

The sixty-three bus comes and we get on. The bus driver says he wasn't expecting to herd up any sheep today. When we've taken our seats and the bus driver can't hear me complaining, I bleat, "That driver's joke was b-aa-aa-aa-d." Billy says I am very funny, but when I ask him why he isn't laughing he says he is, I just can't see it under the balaclava.

The bus takes us down Eden High Street, past the park and houses the colour of Dolly Mixtures and along the seafront where you can see down to the small horseshoe-shaped harbour. Tiny fishing boats bob about like toys in bath water and the slap of the waves against the harbour wall sounds like the rhythm of a heartbeat. We take a sharp turn right and away from the seafront and twenty minutes later we're at Honeydown Hills and it feels like we were only here a few days ago, which we were. My stomach is doing more somersaults than a gymnast, which is stupid because this is our home and Pearl's our "almost" mum. Standing in front of the door I think about what I'm going to say to Pearl when I see her. Maybe I'll just reach out for a hug instead because she's good at giving hugs. I'm sweating like a sheep in a woolly jumper when I eventually take my front door key from my coat pocket. The door opens easily and we both tiptoe into the hallway like two pantomime villains. We stop and listen for voices, but it's quieter than a kebab van outside a vegetarian conference.

"I can't hear Pearl," whispers Billy.

"Me either," I whisper back, running my finger along the blue swallows on the hallway wallpaper. Mum chose that wallpaper. I remember because recently Pearl said she wanted to change it and Dad said Mum picked it and Pearl got in a right huff because she didn't pick it and she was the person living with it. Then she smiled at Dad and said she didn't mind after all and Dad felt guilty about it and said Pearl was right. Dad then said she could change it and Pearl smiled again because that was what she wanted in the first place.

"Oh, Mum," I whisper, my fingers tracing one of the little swallows.

"What?" Billy hisses, lifting up his balaclava. "Did you just say bum?"

I shake my head and say, "Let's hurry up. We can't stay here long because we promised Dad we'd be back for tea." We go into the living room first and immediately Billy says Pearl has gone for good. Following his gaze, I see the ghost of a frame mark on the wall. Pearl's self-portrait that hung above the mantelpiece has disappeared. Pearl painted it one rainy Sunday evening.

"You're right," I reply, staring up at the empty wall. "Pearl wouldn't have taken that down. She loved that portrait."

"Maybe Pearl's moved it upstairs?"

Pearl's self-portrait isn't upstairs; neither is Pearl or any of her stuff. A blade of terror jabs me in the guts and then I realize it's not a blade but Billy's sharp elbow and he's whinging and telling me that this is a real SNOOP mystery but he has an idea where Pearl might have gone. "She's run away to train animals."

"What animals?"

"Unicorns," mumbles Billy. I stare into the slit of the balaclava in case an amoeba with one brain cell has replaced my brother. Nope, it's still Billy.

"Since when have you ever seen a unicorn around here?" I ask Billy, my hands on my hips. Billy tells me he's never seen one but he knows they're all around us because he's seen the evidence. "What evidence?"

"They poop rainbows on the roads," offers Billy.

I think about explaining that's just fuel spills from cars but, seriously, sometimes there is just no point in using all your energy trying to find sense where there is none. Instead I tell Billy this is all pointless and we're going to have to think of something else. Pearl isn't here. "Put the letter on the table downstairs," I say. "If Pearl comes back she'll find it and read it and contact us." It's all I can suggest, unless Billy has any more of his bright ideas.

Billy thinks about it for a moment. "I have a bright idea. How about if I leave the note on Pearl's bed, then if she comes back she'll find it, read it and contact us?"

"Okay, that'll do. Put it there instead," I reply, watching as Billy trots into Dad and Pearl's bedroom with the note clenched between his teeth (which I imagine is quite tricky when you're wearing a thick balaclava). As I wait on the landing for Billy to return,

I see the pencil marks on the side of the airing cupboard door.

They're Mum's pencil marks. Ibiza Nana said she used to put them on the door to see how tall I'd grown. Of course, they stopped when Mum died; just another one of the things that changed. Ibiza Nana took over with the pencil for a bit. After she left, Pearl said she wasn't going to do that because it didn't take a pencil to tell her I was growing when it was costing them a fortune in new clothes and shoes. To hear her, you'd think I was King Kong's bigger brother.

My fingers reach out and touch the pencil marks that Mum made.

I think of her again.

Sadness puddles in my belly, because the last time Mum used the pencil on this wall I bet I thought she'd live with me for ever.

I was wrong.

There's a loud mumbling from Dad and Pearl's bedroom, which translates in balaclavese to: *I have left the note on the bed.*

"Okay then, we'd better go now," I yell back, touching the pencil marks once more. I think about how Mum used to be here in this house with us. And how she'd curl up beside me in the armchair and tell me stories and I'd feel loved and safe and like I was strong enough to take on the world. Ibiza Nana said Mum was the best storyteller in the universe and how she always made sure her stories had a happy-ever-after. Thing is, Mum's own story didn't have a happy-ever-after and I feel a prickling in my eyes as I shout, "Hurry up, Billy, we can't play invisible football much longer. And if Dad comes looking for us we'll be in trouble."

Billy mumbles something else, but this time he's interrupted by a noise downstairs.

A key turns in the lock.

My heart is in my mouth (although technically, I know from all my medical manuals that this is not possible). I yell to Billy to get out here and he comes skidding out of the bedroom. Through the slit in the balaclava, I can see his eyes shimmering like two glitter balls at a disco.

"It's Pearl," mumbles Billy. "It's going to be okay. It's Pear..." Billy's voice trails off into a woolly wilderness as the person in the hallway begins speaking.

It isn't Pearl.